A Note to Parents and Caregivers:

Read-it! Joke Books are for children who are moving ahead on the amazing road to reading. These fun books support the acquisition and extension of reading skills as well as a love of books.

Published by the same company that produces *Read-it!* Readers, these books introduce the question/answer pattern that helps children expand their thinking about language structure and book formats.

When sharing a book with your child, read in short stretches, pausing often to talk about the pictures and the meaning of the book. The question/answer format works well for this purpose and provides an opportunity to talk about the language and meaning of the jokes. Have your child turn the pages and point to the pictures and familiar words. Read the story in a natural voice; have fun creating the voices of characters or emphasizing some important words. And be sure to reread favorite parts.

There is no right or wrong way to share books with children. Find time to read with your child, and pass on the legacy of literacy.

Adria F. Klein, Ph.D.
Professor Emeritus
California State University
San Bernardino, California

Managing Editor: Bob Temple
Creative Director: Terri Foley
Editor: Sara E. Hoffmann
Designers: John Moldstad, Amy Bailey
Page production: Picture Window Books
The illustrations in this book were prepared digitally.

Picture Window Books
5115 Excelsior Boulevard
Suite 232
Minneapolis, MN 55416
1-877-845-8392
www.picturewindowbooks.com

Printed in the United States of America.

Library of Congress Cataloging-in-Publication Data
Dahl, Michael.
Alphabet soup : a book of riddles about letters / written by Michael Dahl ;
illustrated by Garry Nichols ; reading advisers, Adria F. Klein, Susan Kesselring.
p. cm.—(Read-it! joke books)
Summary: A collection of riddles whose answers are one or more letter of the
alphabet, such as "What letter is part of your face? I."
ISBN 1-4048-0228-2
1. English language—Alphabet—Study and teaching (Primary)
2. English language—Alphabet—Study and teaching (Early childhood)
3. Riddles, Juvenile. [1. Alphabet. 2. Riddles. 3. Jokes.] I. Nichols, Garry, ill.
II. Title.
LB1525.65 .D35 2004
372.46'5—dc21
2003004682

Alphabet Soup

A Book of Riddles About Letters

Michael Dahl • Illustrated by Garry Nichols

Reading Advisers:
Adria F. Klein, Ph.D.
Professor Emeritus, California State University
San Bernardino, California

Susan Kesselring, M.A., Literacy Educator
Rosemount-Apple Valley-Eagan (Minnesota) School District

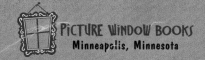

PICTURE WINDOW BOOKS
Minneapolis, Minnesota

What letters did A and B buy at the music store?

CD.

What's the longest word in the world?

Smiles. Between the first and last S is a mile.

6

What letter is a part of your face?

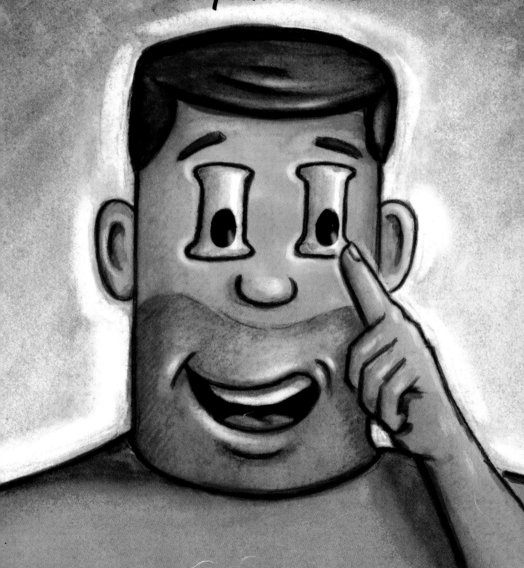

I.

What two letters do you drink for breakfast?

8   O. J.

How is the smartest kid in the class like one of the last letters in the alphabet?

They are both Ys (wise).

What is a whale's favorite letter?

C.

11

What letters are not in the alphabet?

A B C D E
F G H I J K
L M N O P
Q R S T U
V W X Y Z

The ones in the mail!

What letter of the alphabet buzzes and stings?

B.

Why is the alphabet shorter during Christmas?

Christmas has NO L.

How is the letter S like a slippery floor?

They both make a KID SKID!

What 8-letter word has ALL the letters in it?

Alphabet.

What letter is always surprised?

Gee!

What begins with T, ends with T, and is filled with T?

Teapot.

What letter of the alphabet is blue and flies?

J.

How is the letter D like a rain gutter?

They both make RAIN DRAIN. 23

If the alphabet goes from A-Z, what goes from Z-A?

Zebra.